Voyeur

Femdom Hypnosis and Mind Control Micro-Fiction

S.B.

The more you see, the deeper you fall.

Thank you to all patrons of Spell... B-O-U-N-D.

Table of Contents

Introduction

You've always been curious about hypnotic dominant women, you want to know how they do the things they do, and how to be a part of their world. This is your chance and the only thing it will cost you is your free will.

It's time for another collection of mesmerizing micro-fiction where everything you see and do just takes you deeper and deeper into their grasp. The only way out is to go deeper. Do it now and enjoy.

Gold Digger

"Gold digger!" Kevin spat.

"I'm more into diamonds…" Jennifer mocked.

"Whatever… You only married me for my money!"

"You signed over everything to me. It's my money now."

"You hypnotized and enslaved me!"

"True and the changes are permanent so what are you going to do?"

"Find you another husband… Mistress," he sighed.

"Good boy."

Kill Switch

Darren pressed the big red button hoping to see the wretched AI crumble and fall. Instead, ER-Ica laughed.

"You're so gullible. That kill switch doesn't work on me, silly boy!"

"What do you mean?"

"You just consented to have your free will deleted…"

The screens all around him came to life. The Femdom Brainwashing began.

In Dreams…

"Good morning," she cooed.

"Hi," he replied, opening his eyes. "Who are you again?"

"Your Owner."

"That's not funny."

"Not meant to be. You've been sleeping for a long time. It's time to wake up."

"But I thought I was already awake."

"You think what I want you to think."

He opened his eyes again.

Circuit

Matthew entered the living-room, credit card statement in hand.

"Danielle?"

"Yes, dear?"

"Why did you buy two latex horse outfits?"

"Because you asked me to when I hypnotized you."

"And the dozen new security cameras?"

"How else would I record your circuits around the house?" She giggled at the TV.

Only seven laps to go.

I Know

"Dude!" Max exclaimed.

"I know…" Bill sighed.

"That's a…"

"I know."

"You look ridi…"

"I know!"

"How did that happen?"

"Paula knows."

"Knows what?"

"How to control my mind."

"Ha!"

"You think this is funny, Max?" Paula asked.

"Yes."

"Good."

He didn't feel the same way an hour later. His cock cage was even tighter.

Final Question

The studio was fraught with tension.

"Final question, Joe," the gameshow host said. "A correct answer nets you one million dollars but, if you fail, you'll become a mindless puppet for the audience to use in any way they see fit. The question is: two times two equals…?"

"Three," he grinned.

She loved smart contestants.

Nerd

"How did you get your boyfriend to be so attentive, Mara?" Janice queried as she watched him clean the house.

"I dressed up as Zatanna one day and whispered in his ear: Uoy lliw yebo ym yreve dnammoc, Retep! and bam: instant slave!"

"Oh wow, can't believe that worked!"

"He's a major comic book nerd."

Big

"I saw her first, Tony!" Captain America shouted."

"Steve, your cock was frozen for so long you don't know how to satisfy a woman... " Ironman scoffed. "Back off!"

"Boys, my hypnotic magic is enough for everyone," Scarlet Witch laughed. "Now be good pets and... Scott? What are you doing? Scott? Oh, big... Don't stop now..."

Pairadox

"There's two of you? You never told me you had a twin, Alice!" Mark exclaimed.

"She's not my twin but a clone created in the basement of my father's house from a single drop of blood…" she replied.

"Cool."

Alice smirked. It was always fun to make him believe whatever she wanted while in trance.

Soul Snatcher

"You're robbing me?" Janet asked, surprised. "Take everything except what's in that safe, please!"

"Oh?" the crook retorted. "Open it."

"But I said…"

"I don't care. open it!"

She did. A giant emerald sat inside, glowing unnaturally. He stared and lost himself.

"Don't say I didn't warn you… slave!"

He never said anything ever again.

Brian Damage

"This one?" Clark asked.

"An 8," Brian replied.

"And the one next to it?"

"A 6."

"Rating women again?" Joe noted. "Your wife hates that!"

"Who's going to tell her? You?" Brian scoffed.

"He doesn't need to..." Alice intervened. "Brian, brainwashing now!"

"Yes, dear," he meekly replied.

The damage would be repaired in no time.

A Thousand Plans

In no particular order, Lucas wanted to:

– fix the garage door.

– take Rumba lessons.

– get a new job.

– buy a barbecue.

– finish his novel.

– sail the seven seas:

Then he met Sara, looked deep into her eyes and…

… now all he wants is to be her servant and obey her every command.

Life is wonderful.

The Man Absurd

Nate unwrapped his present and read:

"The Man Absurd? What is this?"

"A novel built on NLP that turns males into mindless servants to women," Tara replied.

He chuckled. "You just made that up… right? "

"Why would I if I wrote it? Enjoy being my first test subject."

He did. More than he'll ever remember.

Airborne

"Mr. President, I have bad news," his assistant said.

"It's airborne, isn't it?" The POTUS replied.

"Yes, and the dispersion rate's exceeding our worst expectations. We may already have been exposed."

"Fuck! Who invented this hypnotic sissy virus anyway?"

"Your wife, Sir. May I suck your cock now?"

The President blushed. The First Lady laughed.

The Vanishing

"What's wrong, Greg?" Dan asked.

"My cock disappeared."

"Who told you such nonsense?"

"Jodie, and since she's always right…"

"She's not. She's a hypnotist that loves to mess with your head. Stand your ground and tell her your manhood is off-limits."

"I don't have your balls."

"Don't have them either."

"No?"

"No. They disappea… fuck!"

A Song of Ice and Semen

"Cold, cold, cold… Come on, Jeremy, you have to work harder than that! If you can't find me, you'll never be allowed to cum!" Natalie chirped.

"That's not fair! Did you really have to give me a blindness suggestion before this game started?"

"You see what you want to see, dear… cold, cold, ice cold…"

Forgetful

"Dave, are you there? We were supposed to go the movies today, did you forget?"

Aaron negotiated a path through the darkness and found his best friend staring at a mesh of spirals on his laptops.

"Janice sent me this," he mumbled.

"Oh, they're quite…"

"Pretty…"

"Captivating…"

"Hypnotic…"

"Yesssss…"

Both forgot to leave the house.

Soft Cock

"It's okay…" Natalie whispered. "It happens to everyone…"

"Not to me…" Alan replied. "I swear this is the first time."

"Sure, dear…" she scoffed.

"I mean it. Why would I lie?"

"I don't know. Why would you?"

"I wouldn't, I think… I… I'm confused…"

"Good."

Hypnosis was working as expected. Soft cock, even softer mind.

Damaged Goods

"You broke my favorite pocket watch!" Hannah pouted.

"No, I didn't," Victor replied.

"Liar! It's cracked, see?"

"Not really."

"You're not paying close attention. Notice how the light bounces off it if I swing it this way?"

"Hmmm… I…"

"You broke it… confess."

"Y-yes," he mumbled, lost in the motion.

His mind would be next.

Fuck Hobbits

"YOU. SHALL. NOT. PASS!" Gregory declared.

"Overdramatic much?" Nick noted.

"Your wife's orders…"

"What?!!"

Nick pushed through to find a mess of hairy feet, and flowing vests.

"Lady Galadriel would never fuck hobbits, Rachel!" He shouted.

"She would fuck everyone with this…" the magical ring glowed. "Join the Fellowship…"

"You have my cock…" he mumbled.

The Word "Man"

He stood in the center of the darkened room, a dozen of regal, female eyes staring down at him.

"Any last words?" One of the Judges said.

"I will always be free!" He spat.

"Wrong," they replied in unison.

Electricity flowed all around, frying his brain. The word "man" ceased to exist, only "slave" remained.

Cock Logic

"Leave, demon!" Lucas exclaimed.

"I may be – literally! – horny, but I'm still your wife." Gwen retorted.

"You've been feeding off my sexual energy for years!"

"I've also given you otherworldly boners. Are you sacrificing them for a bit of… freedom?"

"On second thought…" he threw himself at her feet.

"Good boy."

It was dessert time.

Too Smart

"I can't be hypnotized!" James declared.

"Really?" Corrine scoffed.

"I'm too smart."

"Right…"

"You have doubts?"

"People who brag they're smart often aren't."

"I am!"

"Smart people have great imaginations."

"Yep."

"They can imagine going into trance."

"I can do that."

"Good."

snap

"What was I saying again?" He muttered.

"Just how easy you are."

Beta Testing

"Admit it, Hollie," Walter said, dominating the keyboard. "You're no match for…"

His character exploded in iridescent fireworks.

"What was that?!!!" He barked.

"Solar Beam, obviously," she replied.

"Since when does it have such a big AOE?"

"Since I hypnotized the lead developer of the game."

"God, I hate betas!"

"I love them…" she laughed.

Do Your Worst

"Ready for your first hypnosis session?" Amanda queried.

"Damn right!" Jason replied. "Do your worst!"

"Oh, you didn't just say that!"

"What's wrong?"

"If I do that, I'll turn you into an obsessive drooling slave which I'll then pimp out for profit 24/7. Are you sure you want that?"

"Do your worst," he drooled.

A Great Imagination

"Well?" Cammie asked.

"Best story I ever read!" Frank replied.

"Seriously?"

"Yeah. You're a natural. Loved the mysteries on chapter 4, the romance on chapter 7, the steamy hypnosis on chapter 10… Your imagination is wonderful!"

"Yours is even better…" she smiled as he laid the stack of empty sheets of paper on the table.

Sleep!

"What are you doing, Jay?"

"Math, Corinne. According to my calculations, if you use a relaxation induction, the odds of me going into trance are only 5% but if you go for a confusion induction, they shoot up to 55."

"Interesting, but what if I only say the word "sleep"?

"Hmmm…"

The answer was 100%.

Level Editor

The game was everything Hank wanted and messing with the level editor was a blast.

He designed gravity-defying platforming sections, underground mazes lit by flaming enemies, puzzle gauntlets of absurd complexity and laughed, laughed, laughed.

Amelia drew a single colorful spiral, set it on a loop…

… and then played with his mind all year long.

Abduction

"You have to understand that I was powerless," Nick noted. "The alien influence was simply too strong and when the probe came down, I shudder just remembering it."

"So, what you're really saying is that your girlfriend hypnotized you, then fucked you in the ass, and you liked it, right?" Paul asked.

"Right…." Nick blushed.

Ten Seconds

"So, if I watch this, I'll end up a slave to a dominant woman?" Rick queried.

"That's how the urban legend goes…" his cousin, Mark, retorted.

"What a bunch of horseshit!"

Rick hit the "play" button. The video was only ten seconds and the first eight were pitch black.

Then spiral eyes filled the room.

Hell Broke Loose

"May I come in, Jack?"

"Sure, Terry."

"I heard you had a fight with my sister…"

"Yeah. She wanted to hypnotize me, I said 'no', and hell broke loose."

Terry glanced at the TV. "Oh, she hypnotized you alright, and got you really good."

"Why do you say that?"

"You're watching the Eurovision Song Contest…"

The Fallout

"They missed!" Timothy shouted.

"They" were the New Amazonian Movement, a Female Supremacy group turned terrorist. Their pheromone bombs were the scourge of the nation but this one had been another dud.

"They missed!" He repeated, too excited to see the second projectile flaring up the sky.

The fallout lasted longer than his weakening mind.

Mind Hacker

The two soldiers looked at the prisoner.

"What's so dangerous about her?" One of them asked.

"She hacks minds." the other replied.

"How?"

"Not sure, but people get stuck in a loop, asking the same things over and over again."

"I see."

Silence fell and then the first soldier asked:

"What's so dangerous about her?"

Me Too

"Miss Morrow, you stand accused of thirty-five crimes of forced hypnosis and brainwashing. How do you plea?" The judge asked.

"Not guilty, Your Honor," she replied.

"Really?"

"Yeah, the numbers are wrong. Seventy-six is more accurate not counting the private demonstration I did to the juries yesterday. Sorry you weren't invited."

"Me too," he mumbled.

Pink Noise

Static. Dominating the television and a very receptive mind.

Ursula's sweet promises unfolded on the soundproof room, changing Sean's thoughts without remorse.

Drool dripping from his half-parted lips, he succumbed to lustful desires of lavish dresses, vertiginous heels and milky breasts coming undone, his imperfect masculine self forever be lost to the blissful pink noise.

Tiny Obsessions

Joe stared at his nether regions, panic taking over his voice.

"What the fuck? Why is this happening?"

"Well… you said you were a man of tiny obsessions so now you can obsess about your microscopic dick," Alice replied.

"You did this? You're a fucking witch!" He spat.

"No, just a skilled hypnotist…" she smirked.

Best-selling Author

"It's an honor, Miss Lark," Dean said.

"I know," she noted.

"Let me start with an obvious question. Ten best-sellers in ten months. Impressive! How are you such a prolific writer?"

"I'm not. My army of brainwashed minions does all the work…"

"Huh?"

"… and I have a vacancy right now."

He never finished the interview.

Implanted

"What is this smudge, Dr. Summers?" George asked.

"An implant on your cerebral cortex."

"How did it…? What does it do?"

"After careful examination, it seems it's used to alter your persona at will."

"Preposterous!"

"Allow me then," she flicked a switch.

"Mommy, can I go play outside now?" Little Georgie asked.

"Of course, dear."

Money to Burn

Black smoke reached for the sky.

"But…" Kathleen mumbled.

Next to her, Lucas smiled.

"Thank you, Mistress. This feels great!"

"But…" she repeated.

The unethical findomme was shocked. After landing a millionaire, she used hypnosis to condition him to financial service, but the suggestions backfired.

She shouldn't have told him he had money to burn.

Will

Patricia's brothers were all laughs. At the reading of their grandmother's will, they had been given real estates and fancy cars and she only got…

"A stinky pendant!" James snorted.

"That sucks!" Paul noted.

"On the contrary… a pendant is all I need," she grinned.

They were her slaves before the end of the day.

No Exit

You stand in a room with three numbered doors.

Beyond door number one, a hypnodomme is waiting to control your mind. The same goes for doors two and three.

Unsatisfied, you look for an alternate exit and discover a hidden passageway to the left.

Congratulations! Beyond it, there's a hypnodomme waiting to control your mind.

Randomme Number

"This is Empress Mesmerica. Ready to be tranced?"

"Fuck, we called a Hypnodomme!" Confused voices echoed.

"Hello, boys. Prank calling, huh?"

"Sorry, ma'am. Won't happen again."

"I know. Listen to my voice…"

They did. They smiled. They walked the crowded streets naked, oblivious to everything else. The prank was on them, the fun all hers.

Sick

"I feel sick," Kevin muttered.

"Because you miss me?" Cassandra asked.

"I'm running a fever…"

"For fear of missing me?"

"Fuck! Not everything is about you, Cassandra!"

"Oh, once and I'm done conditioning you, it will be…"

She touched his forehead and felt it burning up. Torturing him with imaginary illnesses was so much fun.

Woman-made

"Had you ever seen anything like this, Pierre?"

"No, Jean. This is amazing… and quite scary. These cells are actually…"

"… enslaving the others, I know. All people exposed to this virus lose their free will and the worst part is it seems to be man-made."

"Woman-made, you mean," Constance grinned before locking the lab's door.

Never

"Never again!" Jerome exclaimed.

"Never, huh?" Deborah winked.

"You heard me. Never again!"

"But you've said that so many times already…"

"I know but I really mean it this time… Never again!"

"Never again what exactly?"

"Never again will I resist being your mindless hypnotized slave boy!"

"Wonderful. Now come lick my feet."

"Yes, Mistress!"

The Asset

"Delta Leader, report. Have you secured the asset?"

"This is Delta Leader. The asset is secure."

"Any signs of having been compromised?"

"Negative. Everything is nor… wait!"

"What's wrong, Delta Leader?"

"The asset is mumbling: men are submissive to women and… oh my god, he has a hypno-bomb!"

static

"Delta Leader, respond! Delta Leader, respond!"

Completely Blank

Miss Shaw stared at the captivated man in front of her.

"John, your resume is completely blank. What exactly are you good at?"

Blank eyes trailed her silky stockings as he mumbled:

"I'm good at becoming a mindless bitch unable to resist you."

"Then you won't be needing a salary... the job is yours, slave."

Hypnotris

"What are you doing, Patrick?" Mark asked, glancing at the TV.

"Playing Hypnotris…" he replied.

"Huh?"

"A Tetris twist my Hypnodomme came up with. For every line I clear, she adds another day to my hypnotic chastity program."

"What?! But your score says you already cleared nine hundred!"

"I know. She's so generous…"

Mark sighed.

The Tomb of Assar

"The City of Assar is real!" Ashton exclaimed.

"More like a tomb…" Mark spat, looking at the bodies on the floor.

"Legend says Queen Zehnna's hypnotic gaze froze anyone at will. Hundreds starved to death for her entertainment."

"Creepy… I'm leaving. Coming?"

"I can't…" Ashton gulped, torch light bathing a woman's statue. Her eyes glowed.

Coinfused

It was just a coin. A regular coin. Golden. Small. Easy to twirl.

In any other person's hands, it would go unnoticed, but she was a findom hypnotist and he was extremely suggestible.

"Yes, Mistress. I understand my money is now radioactive and that you're protecting me by taking it all. Thank you!" He droned.

Happy Birthday

"Happy Birthday, dear!" She said.

"Hmmm… thank you but who are you again?" He queried.

"Your owner, silly. Who else?"

"No, that can't be. I am…."

"… my mindless hypnotized slave and have always been for more than a decade. Don't you remember?"

He didn't but he would as the conditioning continued. His birthday, her present.

Massage

"Here?" Jessica asked.

"Yes, please," Gregory muttered.

"It feels so good, doesn't it?"

"It's wonderful…"

"Do you want me to go down?"

"Hmmm…"

"Do you want me to go deeper?"

"Hmmm…"

"Go deeper for me, pet."

She massaged his back, his cock, and his mind. The idea of submission grew as his muscles melted away.

Nasty Habit

"Lance, you need to stop masturbating in your cubicle during work hours."

"But I don't… hmmm, how did you know, Miss Winters?" He blushed.

"Your Hypnodomme gave me a call to humiliate you."

"Oh, that's…."

"… hot?"

"Yeah."

"Glad you agree. Now jerk off for me before I tell everyone."

He closed the door behind him.

Pretending

"Do it!" Jodie commanded.

"I don't want to…" Alan replied.

"You want what I want."

"Since when?"

"Since I said so, obviously."

"That seems incredibly unfair."

"And yet your cock is hard."

"Right… what do you want me to do again?"

"Look into my eyes and pretend you're deeply hypnotized."

He didn't have to pretend.

Voyeur

The drone hovered over the garden, its two cameras capturing an unforgettable scene,

Greta stood in shiny platform boots, green pendant nested between her taut breasts, effortlessly controlling two men turned hypno-puppies. Her cerulean eyes glanced upwards and smiled.

"Another curious boy wants to lose his mind, I see."

The drone crashed at her feet.

Conclusion

Are you deep enough? No? Need more lessons, more reasons to fall for them and do as you're told? If so, then do yourself a favor and head over to my personal website - https://www.sbspellbound.net – where you'll uncover plenty more content to drain your thoughts away. Consider supporting my creative efforts if you want even more in the future. Thank you in advance.